Dog and Mouse

Michelle Nelson-Schmidt

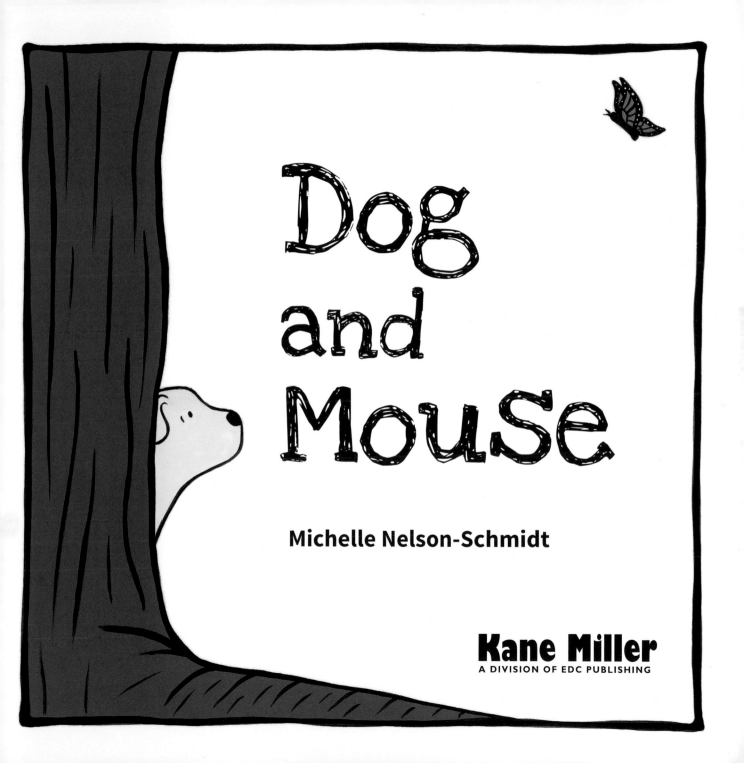

Dog and MouSe

Michelle Nelson-Schmidt

Kane Miller
A DIVISION OF EDC PUBLISHING

Kane Miller, A Division of EDC Publishing

Text and illustrations copyright © Michelle Nelson-Schmidt 2015

For information contact:
Kane Miller, A Division of EDC Publishing
PO Box 470663
Tulsa, OK 74147-0663
www.kanemiller.com
www.edcpub.com
www.usbornebooksandmore.com

Library of Congress Control Number: 2014939757

Printed and bound in Malaysia by Tien Wah Press Pty, Ltd

Hardcover ISBN: 978-1-61067-352-5
Paperback ISBN: 978-1-61067-314-3

For Melinda – who has been my Mouse through it all.
Love you forever, dearest friend.

Out in the woods all the day long,

a little dog searched, beginning at dawn.

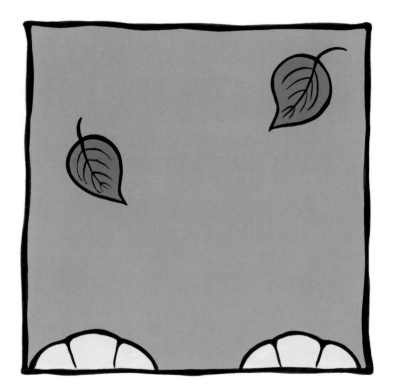

A tiny mouse watched, curious as can be …

… and finally asked what the dog hoped to see.

"I am looking for someone, a very best friend,
who is loyal and true – from beginning to end."

Such a big job! And so important too!
Mouse excitedly offered, "I'll help you!"

What a kind soul, and so very sweet.

Dog thanked Mouse; her help was a treat.

Mouse loved to help. She was just thrilled.
Helping was her favorite and very best skill!

From that moment on, they both met to look,
to find Dog's best friend – whatever it took.

For tall friends and short friends, in the air, on the ground;
they looked everywhere for this friend to be found.

They considered the fact that this friend might stand out,
wearing a cape or a crown would leave little doubt.

Or this friend might be quiet and possibly shy,
one hard to notice, when they passed by.

They looked every day, they looked everywhere,
for all types of friends, this Dog and Mouse pair.

They looked in the morning, from the day's early light,

until the moon and the stars twinkled at night.

And no matter what, Mouse came to the woods,

for no other reason, except that she could.

Every day for a year, they were always a pair,
except for the day … when Mouse *wasn't* there.

"Where is that Mouse?" Dog wondered aloud.
"She was good at looking." Mouse made Dog proud.

Dog thought of the ways that Mouse made her laugh,

the moments they shared as time quickly passed.

They'd smiled and played,
their days filled with fun,

because that dear Mouse
always would come.

Dog soon realized just how much
that she cared,

the more the time passed
without that Mouse there.

So Dog set off to find Mouse – but then wait!
That Mouse – she showed up. She was just late!

Looking at Mouse, it was then that Dog knew.
MOUSE was the one, it had *always* been true.

And that little Mouse, upon learning this fact,
was truly surprised and taken aback.

Because Mouse had just done what she knew that she should:
helping out someone just because that she *could*.

Sometimes the thing that you just cannot see
is right in front of you, clear as can be.

Make this a personal audio book!

To get started:
1. Download the free StorySticker app, or visit www.storysticker.com
2. Set up an account
3. Scan or enter the code below
4. Record yourself reading the story one page at a time and save when finished

Great for any child to read along with parents, grandparents or whomever they choose!

WSZJBTXXY